Tips for Reading Together

Children learn best when reading is fun.

- Talk about the title and the pictures on the cover.
- Discuss what you think the story might be about.
- Read the story together, inviting your child to read as much of it as they can.
- Give lots of praise as your child reads, and help them when necessary.
- Try different ways of helping if they get stuck on a word. For example, get them to say the first sound of the word, or break it into chunks, or read the whole sentence again, trying to guess the word. Focus on the meaning.
- Have fun finding the clocks and watches in the pictures. Read the times together.
- Re-read the story later, encouraging your child to read as much of it as they can.

Children enjoy re-reading stories and this helps to build their confidence.

Have fun!

Find all the clocks and watches in the pictures.

The Lost Voice

Written by Cynthia Rider

Illustrated by Alex Brychta

OXFORD

UNIVERSITY PRESS

Chip didn't feel very well. His throat
was sore and he couldn't talk.

"Chip has lost his voice," said Dad.

"Oh no!" thought Floppy.

Mum took Chip to the doctor.

Dad took Biff and Kipper to school.

Floppy was all on his own.

"Chip has lost his voice," he thought sadly. "I wish I could help him."

"I know!" thought Floppy.
"I'll go and find Chip's
voice. I'm good at
finding things."

He wagged his tail
and ran upstairs.

Floppy ran into Chip's bedroom.
He looked under the bed. He found
a ball, a toy car, a sticky sweet and
a dusty sock . . .

. . . but he didn't find
Chip's lost voice.

Floppy looked in the toy box.
He found lots of toys and lots
of books . . .

. . . but he didn't find
Chip's lost voice.

Suddenly, the phone rang.
"There are voices in the phone,"
thought Floppy. "I bet Chip's voice
is in there."

Floppy hit the phone with his paw.
CRASH! It fell down. A voice said,
"Hello! Is anyone there?"

But it wasn't Chip's voice.

Floppy looked at the radio. "There are voices in the radio," he thought. "I bet Chip's voice is in there."

He hit the radio with his paw.
Nothing happened. He hit it harder
. . . and harder!

CRASH! The radio fell over
and someone started to sing.
"What a horrible noise," thought
Floppy. "That isn't Chip."

"I bet Chip's voice is in the television," thought Floppy. He ran to look. His paw hit the switch and the television came on.

Floppy saw a dog on the television.
It ran out of a shop with a big bone.
"Wow! That bone looks good,"
thought Floppy.

The dog ran faster and faster. A voice shouted, "Stop! Stop that dog!"

"That isn't Chip," thought Floppy, and he went back upstairs.

Floppy saw Teddy on Kipper's bed.
"Teddy!" he thought. "I bet Teddy
has got Chip's voice."

Floppy shook Teddy hard.
Grrrrrrr! growled Teddy.
"Help!" barked Floppy. He dropped
Teddy and ran into Biff's bedroom.

WHOOSH! Floppy went skidding across the floor.

CRASH! Biff's clock fell over. "Wake up!" it shouted.

Floppy was scared. He hid under
Chip's bed and shut his eyes. Soon,
he was fast asleep.

Chip came home. He was feeling
a lot better now.

"Where are you, Floppy?" he called.

Floppy jumped up. "Chip has found his voice!" he thought.

He wagged his tail and ran downstairs.

Just then, Biff came in. Her throat
was sore and she couldn't talk.

"Biff has lost her voice," said Dad.

"Oh no!" thought Floppy.

Think about the story

Why did Dad say that Chip had lost his voice?

Where did Floppy look for Chip's voice?

What do you think happened next?

What would Floppy find if he looked under your bed?

Hidden words

Help Floppy to get his bone by finding the words hidden within the words on the stairs, like this: h**is**

sticky

crash

Biff

growl

clock

shout

stop

has

his

Useful common words repeated in this story and other books in the series. are came couldn't didn't find found harder isn't over saw talk thought under upstairs with

Names in this story: Mum Dad Biff Chip Kipper Floppy

More books for you to enjoy

Level 1:
Getting Ready

Level 2:
Starting to Read

Level 3:
Becoming a Reader

Level 4:
Building Confidence

Level 5:
Reading with Confidence

OXFORD
UNIVERSITY PRESS

Great Clarendon Street,
Oxford OX2 6DP

Text © Cynthia Rider 2006
Illustrations © Alex Brychta 2006
This edition published 2010

First published 2006
All rights reserved

Read at Home Series Editors:
Kate Ruttle, Annemarie Young

British Library Cataloguing
in Publication Data available

ISBN: 9780198387688

10 9 8 7 6 5 4 3 2 1

Printed in China by Imago

Have more fun
with Read at Home